Thomas
Bond

CHILDREN'S STORYTIME TREASURY

Just-So Stories

A PARRAGON BOOK

PUBLISHED BY PARRAGON BOOK SERVICE LTD.
UNITS 13-17, AVONBRIDGE TRADING ESTATE, ATLANTIC ROAD,
AVONMOUTH, BRISTOL BS11 9QD

PRODUCED BY THE TEMPLAR COMPANY PLC,
PIPPBROOK MILL, LONDON ROAD, DORKING, SURREY RH4 1JE

COPYRIGHT © 1996 PARRAGON BOOK SERVICE LIMITED

ILLUSTRATED BY JO CAINE

DESIGNED BY MARK KINGSLEY-MONKS

PRINTED AND BOUND IN SPAIN

ISBN 0-75252-038-5

CHILDREN'S STORYTIME TREASURY

Just-So Stories

·PARRAGON·

HOW THE LEOPARD GOT HIS SPOTS

Long, long ago, the Leopard and the Ethiopian lived in a 'sclusively bare, hot and sandy-yellow-brownish place called the High Veldt. The Giraffe and the Zebra lived there too and they were 'sclusively sandy-yellow-brownish all over. But not as sandy-yellow-brownish as the Leopard and the Ethiopian. The Leopard would lie down behind a brownish rock and the Ethiopian would hide behind a clump of yellowish grass and when the Giraffe or the Zebra would come by, they would leap out of their hiding places and give them the fright of their jumpsome lives. Indeed they would!

After a long time the Giraffe and the Zebra learnt to stay away from the parts of the High Veldt that could be hiding a Leopard or an Ethiopian and they began to look for somewhere else to live.

The Giraffe and the Zebra went to the forest. It was quite different from the High Veldt for it was full of stripy, speckly, patchy-blatchy shadows and there they hid safe from harm. After an even longer time (things lived for ever so long in those days), what with standing in the slippery-slidy shadows of the trees, the Giraffe grew blotchy and the Zebra grew stripy.

By now the Leopard and the Ethiopian had grown very hungry and so they asked Baviaan, the wise Baboon, where the other animals had gone.

"They decided it was high time for a change and they have gone into other spots and my advice to you, Leopard, is to do the same." Then the Leopard and the Ethiopian searched the forest but although they could smell them and they could hear them, to their great surprise they found they could not see the animals.

Soon it grew dark, and then the Leopard heard something breathing sniffily quite near him. It smelt like Zebra and when he stretched out his paw it felt like Zebra. So the Leopard jumped out of his tree and sat on this strange thing until morning because there was something about it that he didn't quite like.

Presently he heard a grunt and a crash and he heard the Ethiopian call out.

"I've caught a thing that I cannot see. It smells like Giraffe and it kicks like Giraffe but it hasn't any shape."

"Don't trust it," advised the Leopard. "Just sit on its head till the morning comes, same as me." So there they sat and waited until the sun rose for then the light would show them just what they had caught.

At sunrise the Leopard looked over at the Ethiopian.

"What have you got down your end of the table, Brother?" he asked. The Ethiopian scratched his head.

"Well, it ought to be Giraffe, but it is covered all over with chestnut blotches. What have you got?"

"Well, it ought to be Zebra," replied the Leopard, equally puzzled, "but it's covered all over with black stripes. What have you both been doing to yourselves?"

Then the Giraffe and the Zebra stood up.

"Watch us disappear," they said and they walked off towards some tall bushes where the shadows fell all blotchy and stripy. "This is the way it's done. One, two, three, where's your breakfast?" The Leopard stared and the Ethiopian stared but all they could see were stripy shadows and blotchy shadows.

"That's a lesson worth learning!" declared the Ethiopian. "I'm going to change myself, too. I want to be a nice blackish-brownish colour. It will be the very thing for hiding in hollows and behind trees." So he changed his skin then and there and when he had finished he spoke to his friend. "You should take Baviaan's advice, Leopard, and go into other spots, too."

"Very well," decided the Leopard, "but don't make 'em too vulgar-big. I wouldn't look like Giraffe - not for ever so." So the Ethiopian pressed his fingertips all over the Leopard and soon he was covered in spots.

Wherever the Ethiopian's five fingers touched his coat, they left five little black marks, all close together. Sometimes his fingers slipped and the marks got a little blurred, but if you look closely at any Leopard now you will see that there are always five spots — off five fat black fingertips.

"Now you can lie out on the ground and look like a heap of pebbles," said the Ethiopian. "You can lie on a leafy branch and look like dappled sunshine. Think of that and purr!"

And so the animals were very proud of their new coats and were very glad that they had changed. Oh, one last thing. Now and again you will hear grown-ups say, "Can the Leopard change his spots?" I don't think even grown-ups would keep on saying such a silly thing if the Leopard hadn't done it once — do you? But they will never do it again, Best Beloved. Oh no, they are quite contented just as they are.

HOW THE RHINOCEROS GOT HIS SKIN

Once upon a time on the shores of the Red Sea there lived a Parsee from whose hat the rays of the sun were reflected in more-than-oriental splendour. One day the Parsee baked a splendid fruit cake upon his stove.

But to his great dismay down to the beach from the Altogether Uninhabited Interior came a Rhinoceros with a horn on his nose, two piggy eyes, and few manners. In those days the Rhinoceros's skin fitted him quite tight. There were no wrinkles in it anywhere. When the Parsee saw him coming, he climbed to the top of the nearest palm tree for he knew that the Rhinoceros had no manners whatever.

Then the Rhinoceros upset the stove and he spiked that cake on the end of his horn and he ran off with it across the sand. When he had disappeared, the Parsee climbed down from his tree and solemnly recited this short verse:

> *"Them that takes cakes*
> *Which the Parsee man bakes*
> *Makes dreadful mistakes."*

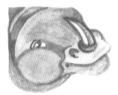

Five weeks later there was a heatwave in the Red Sea, and everybody took off all the clothes they had. The Parsee took off his hat and the Rhinoceros took off his skin and carried it over his shoulder as he went down to the beach to bathe. In those days it buttoned underneath with three buttons and looked a bit like a raincoat. He carefully laid his skin on the sand and waddled straight into the water where he had great fun blowing huge bubbles through his nose.

Presently the Parsee came by and found the skin, and he smiled a smile that ran all round his face two times. Then he went to his camp and filled his hat with cake-crumbs (for he had baked another cake). Next he took the Rhinoceros skin and he scrubbed and rubbed that skin just as full of old, dry, stale, tickly cake-crumbs as ever it could possibly hold.

Then he climbed to the top of his palm tree and
waited for the Rhinoceros to come out of the water
and put on his skin. And the Rhinoceros did. He
buttoned it up with the three buttons, and it tickled
like cake crumbs in bed. Then he wanted to scratch,
but that made it worse. So he lay down on the sand and
rolled and rolled and rolled, and every time he rolled,
the crumbs tickled him worse and worse and worse.

Then he ran to the palm tree and rubbed and rubbed
and rubbed himself against it. He rubbed so much and
so hard that he rubbed his skin into a great fold over
his shoulders, and another fold underneath where the
buttons used to be, and he rubbed some more folds
over his legs.

But it didn't make any difference to the cake crumbs.
They were inside his skin and they tickled. High up at
the very top of his palm tree, the Parsee hugged
himself and smiled a satisfied smile.

At last the rhinoceros gave up scratching and rolling
on the sand and rubbing on the tree and he went
home, very angry indeed and horribly scratchy, and
from that day to this every rhinoceros has great folds in
his skin and a very bad temper, all on account of the
cake crumbs inside.

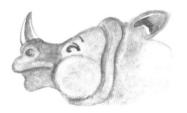

HOW THE WHALE GOT HIS THROAT

In the sea, once upon a time, was a Whale, and he ate fishes. He ate the starfish and the garfish, and the crab and the dab, and the plaice and the dace, and the skate and his mate and the mackerel and the pickereel and the really truly twirly-whirly eel. All the fishes he could find in the sea he ate with his mouth till at last there was only one small fish left, and he was a 'Stute Fish, and he swam just behind the Whale's ear so as to be out of harm's way.

"I'm hungry," complained the Whale at last. Then the 'Stute Fish said in a small 'Stute voice, "Noble and generous Cetacean, have you ever tasted Man? Man tastes nice. A bit nubbly — but nice."

"Then fetch me some," said the Whale.

"If you swim to latitude Fifty North, longitude Forty West (that is Magic), you will find, sitting on a raft, in the middle of the sea, wearing green canvas breeches and strong red braces, one shipwrecked Mariner, who, it is only fair to tell you, is a man of infinite-resource-and-sagacity," said the Fish.

Then the Whale swam to the very spot and there he swallowed the Mariner and the raft he was sitting upon and so the Mariner found himself truly inside the Whale's warm, dark inside cupboards. There he jumped and stumped and thumped and humped and he pranced and danced and banged and clanged and he hit and bit and he prowled and howled and he crawled and bawled, until the Whale felt most unhappy indeed.

"This man is very nubbly, and besides he is making me hiccough," complained the Whale to the 'Stute Fish. "I am going to get rid of him."

Then the Whale swam over the sea to the shore and he rushed halfway up the beach and opened his mouth. But while the Whale had been swimming, the Mariner had cut his raft into a square grating and he had tied it firmly inside the Whale's throat with his braces!

Then out he jumped onto the beach and spoke:

"By means of a grating I have stopped your ating."

And it was true. The Whale could no longer eat big fish or men. No, from then on all he could eat was the very smallest of tiny fish for only the smallest of fish could pass through the holes in the grating.

How the Camel got his Hump

Now this tale tells how the Camel got his big hump. In the beginning of years, when he world was so new-and-all, and the Animals were just beginning to work for Man, there lived a Camel, and he lived in the middle of a Howling Desert because he did not want to work.

He ate thorns and tamarisks and milkweed and prickles and was most 'scruciating idle, and when anybody spoke to him he said "Humph!" Just "Humph!" and no more. The Dog and the Horse and the Ox each tried to persuade him to help them with the work but the Camel would only reply "Humph!" Now the other animals thought that this was most unfair so when one day the Djinn of All Deserts came rolling along in a cloud of dust (Djinns always travel that way because it is Magic), they asked for help.

"Djinn of All Deserts," said the Horse, "is it right for any one to be idle, with the world so new-and-all? There is a thing in the middle of your Howling Desert with a long neck and long legs and he won't do a stroke of work."

Then the Djinn rolled across the desert until he found the Camel most 'scruciatingly idle, looking at his own reflection in a pool of water.

"You have given the Horse, the Dog and the Ox extra work, all on account of your 'scruciating idleness," said the Djinn sternly to the Camel.

"Humph!" the Camel replied.

"I shouldn't say that again if I was you," said the Djinn, and he began to work a Magic. Then the Camel said "Humph!" again; but no sooner had he said it than he saw his back begin to puff up and puff up into a great big lolloping humph.

"That is your very own humph that you have brought upon your very own self by not working," said the Djinn. "In future you will be able to work and work and work for three whole days at a stretch without ever having to stop and eat, because now you can live off your humph."

Then the Camel humphed himself, humph and all, and went away to join the three Animals. And from that day to this the Camel always wears a Humph (but we call it a "hump" now, so as not to hurt his feelings).

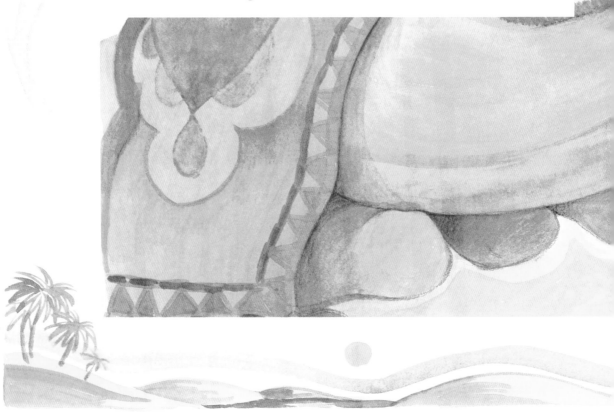

The Elephant's Child

In the High and Far-Off Times the Elephant, O Best Beloved, had no trunk. He had only a blackish, bulgy nose, as big as a boot, that he could wriggle about from side to side, but he couldn't pick up things with it. Now there was one Elephant, a new Elephant, an Elephant's Child, who was full of 'satiable curiosity — and that means he asked ever so many questions. *And* he lived in Africa and he filled all Africa with his 'satiable curtiosities.

He asked his tall aunt, the Ostrich, why her tail-feathers grew just so. He asked his tall uncle, the Giraffe, what made his skin spotty. He asked his broad aunt, the Hippopotamus, why her eyes were red and he asked his hairy uncle, the Baboon, why melons tasted just so. He asked questions about everything that he saw, or heard, or felt, or smelt, or touched, and his aunts and his uncles spanked and spanked him but *still* he was full of 'satiable curiosity!

One fine morning the Elephant's Child asked a new fine question that he had never asked before.

"What does the Crocodile have for dinner?" he said. Then everybody said "Hush!" and spanked him well.

When they had quite finished, the Elephant's Child
came upon Kolokolo Bird sitting in a thorn bush.
"If you want to find out what the Crocodile has for
dinner," said the Bird, "you must go to the banks of
the great grey-green, greasy Limpopo River, all set
about with fever-trees, and there you will find out."
So the Elephant's Child set off to find the Crocodile.
Now you must understand, O Best Beloved, that this
'satiable Elephant's Child had never seen a
Crocodile, and did not know what one was like.

But nevertheless he set off for the Limpopo River and the first thing that he found was a Bi-Coloured-Python-Rock-Snake curled round a rock.

"'Scuse me," said the Elephant's Child most politely, "but have you seen such a thing as a Crocodile in these promiscuous parts?"

Then the Bi-Coloured-Python-Rock-Snake uncoiled himself very quickly from the rock, and spanked the Elephant's Child with his scalesome, flailsome tail, and when he had finished the Elephant's Child thanked him politely and continued on his way.

After a while he trod on what he thought was a log of wood at the very edge of the great grey-green, greasy Limpopo River, but it was really the Crocodile, O Best Beloved, and the Crocodile winked one eye — like this!

"'Scuse me," said the Elephant's Child most politely, "but do you happen to have seen a Crocodile in these promiscuous parts?"

Then the Crocodile winked the other eye, and lifted half his tail out of the mud, and the Elephant's Child stepped back most politely, because he did not wish to be spanked again.

"Come hither, Little One," said the Crocodile. "Why do you ask me such things?"

"'Scuse me," said the Elephant's Child, "but all my aunts and uncles have spanked me and the Bi-Coloured-Python-Rock-Snake has spanked me and so, if it's all the same to you, I don't want to be spanked again."

"Come hither, Little One," said the Crocodile, "for I am the Crocodile," and he wept crocodile-tears to show it was quite true. Then the Elephant's Child grew all breathless, and panted, and then he spoke.

"You are the very person I have been looking for all these long days. Will you please tell me what you have for dinner?"

"Come hither, Little One," said the Crocodile, "and I'll whisper."

Then the Elephant's Child put his head down close to the Crocodile's musky, tusky mouth, and the Crocodile caught him by his little nose, which up to that moment had been no bigger than a boot.

"I think," said the Crocodile from between his teeth, like this, "I think today I will begin with Elephant's Child!" and he pulled and he pulled and he pulled.

"Led go!" said the Elephant's Child. "You are hurtig me!" Then the Bi-Coloured-Python-Rock-Snake scuffled down the bank and knotted himself in a double-clove-hitch around the Elephant's Child's legs.

And he pulled, and the Elephant's Child pulled, and the Crocodile pulled — but the Elephant's Child and the Bi-Coloured-Python-Rock-Snake pulled hardest (and by this time the poor nose was nearly five feet long!)

At last the Crocodile let go of the Elephant's Child's nose with a plop that you could hear all up and down the Limpopo. Then the Elephant's child dangled his poor pulled nose in the water.

"I am waiting for it to shrink," he explained.

There he sat for three days patiently waiting for his nose to shrink back to its usual size but the long stretched nose never grew any shorter. For, O Best Beloved, you will see and understand that the Crocodile had pulled it out into a really truly trunk same as all Elephants have today.

At the end of the third day a fly came and stung him on the shoulder and before he knew what he was doing he lifted up his trunk and hit that fly dead with the end of it. Later he grew hungry, so almost without thinking he put out his trunk and plucked a large bundle of grass and stuffed it in his mouth.

"The sun is very hot here," said the Elephant's Child, and before he thought what he was doing he schlooped up a schloop of mud from the banks of the river and he slapped it on his head where it made a cool schloopy-sloshy mud cap all trickly behind his ears.

Then the Elephant's Child went home across Africa and how proud he was of his useful new nose. And the first thing he did when he saw all his relations was to spank them with his long trunk — and after that, none of them dared spank anyone ever again!

THE CAT THAT WALKED BY HIMSELF

Hear and attend; for this befell and behappened, O Best Beloved, when the Tame animals were wild. The Dog was wild, and the Horse was wild, and the Cow was wild, and the Sheep was wild, and the Pig was wild — as wild as wild could be — and they all walked in the Wet Wild Woods by their wild lones.

But the wildest of all the wild animals was the Cat. He walked by himself and all places were alike to him.

Of course the Man was wild too. He was dreadfully wild. He didn't even begin to be tame till he met the Woman, and she told him that she did not like living in his wild ways.

So she found a nice dry cave to lie down in and she lit a nice fire of wood at the back of the cave. Then she hung a dried wild-horse skin across the opening of the cave, and she said, "Wipe your feet, dear, when you come in, and now we'll keep house."

That night as the Man slept by the fire, the Woman sat up combing her hair. She took the bone of a shoulder of mutton and she looked at the wonderful marks that were carved on it and she made the First Singing Magic in the world. Out in the Wet Wild Woods the wild animals could see the bright light of the fire and they wondered what it meant.

Wild Dog lifted up his head and said, "I will go up and see and look. Cat, come with me."

"Nenni!" said the Cat. "I am the Cat who walks by himself, and all places are alike to me. I will not come." But after Wild Dog had set off, the Cat secretly followed him and hid himself where he could see everything.

Wild Dog entered the cave and sniffed the beautiful smell of the roast mutton and the Woman laughed.

"Here comes the first. Wild Thing out of the Wild Woods, what do you want?"

Wild Dog said, "O my Enemy and Wife of my Enemy, what is this that smells so good in the Wild Woods?" Then the Woman gave him the bone to gnaw and it was so delicious that he wanted another.

"Wild Thing out of the Wild Woods," said the Woman. "Help my Man to hunt through the day and guard this cave at night, and I will give you as many bones as you need." And so the Wild Dog became the First Friend.

"Ah!" said the Cat, listening. "This is a very wise Woman, but she is not so wise as I am."

The next night the Woman made a Second Magic and this time the Wild Horse went to see the strange light.

The Cat followed very softly and watched him enter the cave. The Woman laughed and said, "Here comes the second. Wild Thing out of the Wild Woods, what do you want?" Then the Wild Horse looked at the sweet grass that lay in a mound on the floor of the cave.

"Bend your head and wear this halter," said the Woman, "and you shall eat the grass three times a day."

"Ah!" said the Cat. "This is a clever Woman, but she is not so clever as I am."

When the Man and the Dog came back from hunting, the Man said, "What is Wild Horse doing here?"

And the Woman said, "He is now the First Servant and he will carry us from place to place for always."

The next day the Woman made her Third Magic and this time the Wild Cow came up to the cave and she promised to give her milk to the Woman every day in return for the wonderful grass. The Cat went back through the Wet Wild Woods and he never told anybody what he had seen.

But in the morning he went back to the cave and he saw the light of the fire and he smelt the warm milk. Then the Woman laughed and said, "Wild Thing out of the Wild Woods, go away for I have put away the magic bone, and we have no more need of either friends or servants in our cave."

Cat said, "I am not a friend, and I am not a servant. I am the Cat who walks by himself, and I wish to come in."

"No," said the Woman. "If you are the Cat who walks by himself, all places are alike to you. Go away and walk by yourself in all places alike." But the Cat liked the warm cave and he spoke again.

"You are very wise and beautiful," he said. "You should not be cruel, even to a Cat." Then the Woman laughed.

"I knew I was wise, but I did not know I was beautiful. So I will make a bargain with you. If ever I say one word in your praise, you may come into the cave. And if ever I say two words in your praise, you may sit by the fire. And if ever I say three words in your praise, you may drink the warm milk for always and always."

Cat went far away and hid himself in the Wet Wild Woods by his wild lone for a long time till the Woman forgot all about him. Only the Bat that hung upside down in the cave knew where the Cat had hidden himself and one evening he brought news.

"There is a Baby in the cave. He is new and pink and fat and small, and the Woman is very fond of him."

The next morning the Cat found the Baby sitting outside the cave. The Woman was busy cooking but the Baby's cries kept interrupting her. Then the Cat put out his paddy paw and patted the Baby on the cheek and the Baby laughed. The Woman heard him and smiled.

"A blessing on that Wild Thing who is playing with my Baby," said the Woman. "I am very busy and whoever he is, he is helping me by keeping the Baby happy." Then the horse-skin curtain fell down at the mouth of the cave and the Cat strolled inside and sat down. The Woman was very angry to see the Cat inside the cave but she knew that the bargain had to be kept. The Baby began to cry once more and this time the Cat purred a gently lullaby in its ear until it fell fast asleep.

"You are certainly very clever, O Cat," said the Woman.

Then the smoke suddenly puffed up from the fire and when it had cleared, there sat the Cat sitting quite comfy close to the heat of the flames.

"Now I can sit by the warm fire for always and always," said the Cat, "but still I am the Cat who walks by himself, and all places are alike to me." But the Woman was very angry and promised herself she would not say a third word in praise of the Cat.

By and by the cave grew so still that a little mouse crept out of a corner and ran across the floor.

"Ouh! Chee!" cried the Woman, and she jumped upon a stool. Then the Cat made one pounce and caught the little mouse in his claws.

"A hundred thanks," said the Woman. "You must be very wise to catch a mouse so easily."

Then the Milk-pot crackled in two pieces and lo and behold! the Cat was lapping up the warm white milk!

That evening the Man and the Dog were displeased to see the Cat in their cave. The Man took off his two leather boots and he set them in a row with his stone axe, a piece of wood and a hatchet.

"This is our bargain," he said. "If you do not catch mice in the cave for always and always, I will throw these five things at you whenever I see you, and so shall all proper men do after me."

"And if you are not kind to the Baby," added the Dog, "then I will hunt you and try to bite you. And so shall all proper Dogs do after me."

But the Cat was not worried. "*Still* I am the Cat who walks by himself, and all places are alike to me."

Then the Man and the Dog were angry and they chased him up a tree. And from that moment to this three proper men out of five will always throw things at a Cat, and all proper Dogs will chase him up a tree.

But between times, and when the moon gets up and night comes, he is the Cat that walks by himself, and all places are alike to him.